S0-AVI-706

Published 2014 by Satiama, LLC
(www.satiama.com)
PO Box 1397
Palmer Lake, CO 80133
719-487-0424

Published and distributed by Satiama, LLC
(www.satiama.com)

ISBN: 978-0-9832687-5-8

Story, illustrations, and graphic design by Susan Andra Lion
Copyright 2014, Susan Andra Lion and Satiama, LLC
All art and illustrations may not be reproduced by any means, whether electronic or
otherwise, without first obtaining written permission from Satiama, LLC (www.satiama.com)

ALL RIGHTS RESERVED. No part of this book may be reproduced or transmitted
by any mechanical, photographic or electronic process or in any form of a phonographic
recording; nor may it be stored in a retrieval system, transmitted, or otherwise be copied
for public or private use – other than for "fair use" as brief quotations embodied in
articles and reviews – without prior written permission of the publisher, Satiama, LLC.
The intent of the author is only to offer information of a general nature to help you and
your children in your quest for appreciation of and learning about the Earth and its
inhabitants in many forms. The author and publisher assume no responsibility for the
use of the information in this book, whether for yourself or on behalf of others.

PRINTED IN CHINA

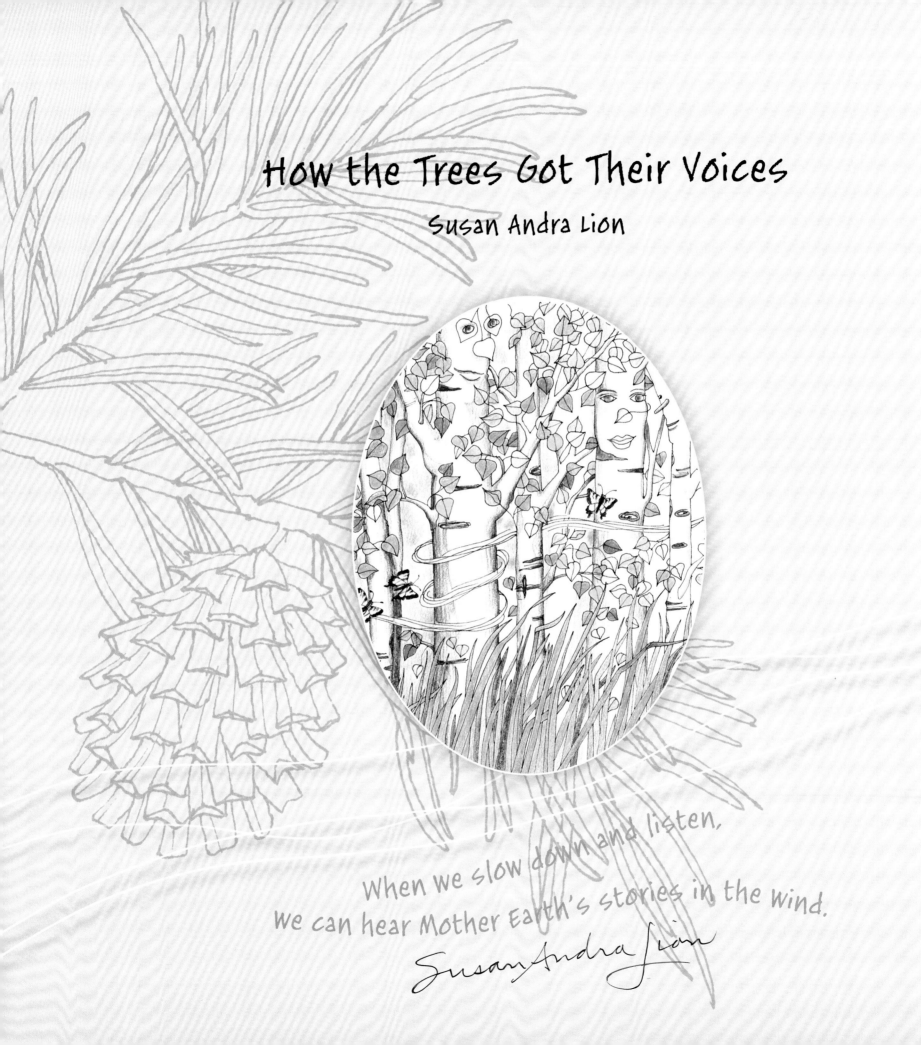

How the Trees Got Their Voices

Susan Andra Lion

When we slow down and listen,
we can hear Mother Earth's stories in the wind.

Susan Andra Lion

There are good reasons to get to know trees. They are the beacons

of our earth, standing tall in rain, wind, and sunshine. They

provide amazing gifts for innumerable creatures, from bugs to birds

to bears. They hold down the earth, provide shade, and sing to us in

the wind. Sometimes they bloom, sometimes wear brilliant colors,

and sometimes offer their branches for treehouses and swings.

So, it's time to get to know your neighbors, the trees.

Have FUN!

Dear Friends,

This book is really a set of two stories. We recommend that you first read the story
of the trees and their remarkable gifts. Then, we suggest you read the book again
to enjoy all the facts around the edges about the animals and the earth.
Thank you for allowing me to share my experience with you of How The Trees Got Their Voices!

Much Love, Susan Andra Lion

To my daughters, Robyn and Brooke –
I thank you for allowing me to read to you
all those years.

And thanks to my sister Kadie, and my numerous friends and colleagues for encouraging me to get this story finished. I'm forever grateful for your helpful and loving advice.

Long-Eared Owl sleeps during the day and hunts at night. Good thing chipmunks sleep at night.

Chipmunks love fruit and nuts. Maybe they are looking for crumbs left by the kids.

Red Fox is curious – and patient. She is careful to move quietly, and because of that, she is a successful hunter.

Fires are used for cooking, toasting marshmallows, and heat, but they are also lovely to sit around and sing.

Believe me, magic can happen ... when it's most unexpected.

A bunch of kids and I were having a lot of fun camping. The wind had raced through the pines all night, rattling tent flaps and nerves.

Downy Woodpecker, looking for lunch, sounds like a drum while pecking at bugs in the bark!

Cottonwood trees can live to be 100 years old.

Raccoons are rascals, and very curious. Their hands are very sensitive so they can get into places quickly and easily.

Blue Jay is a noisy bird and has lots of different calls and cries. It eats seeds, fruit, and insects, and even mice and fish.

Fires should only be built in fire circles where fires are allowed. And someone must tend to the fire at all times.

Telling stories and singing with your friends, in the woods, in a tent, is really fun. Do you have a favorite outdoor story?

So, with breakfast cooked earlier and pocket lunches consumed, the girls took a break in their tent. As they started singing their favorite songs, I settled down near the fire circle with a wildflower book. The sun was bright but I pulled my jacket close to squeeze in a little more heat.

Little did I know that a touch of magic had begun.

If the wind spoke to you, what would it say? Wind has its own stories to share with the lucky person who slows down to listen.

A bandana is sometimes called a "109" because it has a 109 uses. It can hold interesting rocks, handle hot pans, and be used as a hat. Can you think of 109 uses for your bandana?

I began to hear low, musical voices. They were so quiet, my ears squinted to hear the words.

White Tail Deer listen and smell the wind. Is there any sign of danger? The little fawn sleeps peacefully – all is well.

These hardy purple Lupines grow in pine and aspen forests and in open meadows.

The sounds came again and again.

Suddenly, I realized the words were not from people!

I moved my eyes to the stately trees standing together like families – tall and small, all laughing and chattering in the wind.

Quaking Aspens shimmer in the wind, like silver dollars. An aspen is the largest plant living on the planet, and the biggest one is in Colorado.

Red Squirrel feasts on squaw bush berries and tucks the extras in its cheeks.

Curious Raccoon is checking to see if anyone wants to play hide and seek. Do you think her mask will hide her?

Black Bear cub is looking for a friend – or food – whatever comes first. He clambers over rocks, sniffing out the ripe berries.

Red Breasted Nuthatch hops headfirst down the trunk of the tree looking for bugs.

I carefully picked my way through some wildflowers to a knobby rock outcropping. It was home to pines, aspens, squaw bush, and a bunch of curious animals and twittering birds.

Red-Tailed Hawk lives high on a rocky ledge. It is swooping low, checking out who is staying at the campsite.

Tents come in all shapes and sizes. I sleep in one that's not tall enough to stand up in and is light enough to carry in a backpack. Very cozy!

Blue Columbine like sunshine and also the heat a big rock gives off on a chilly night.

Magical voices swirled and twirled all around me.

They whispered in my ears and played with my curiosity.

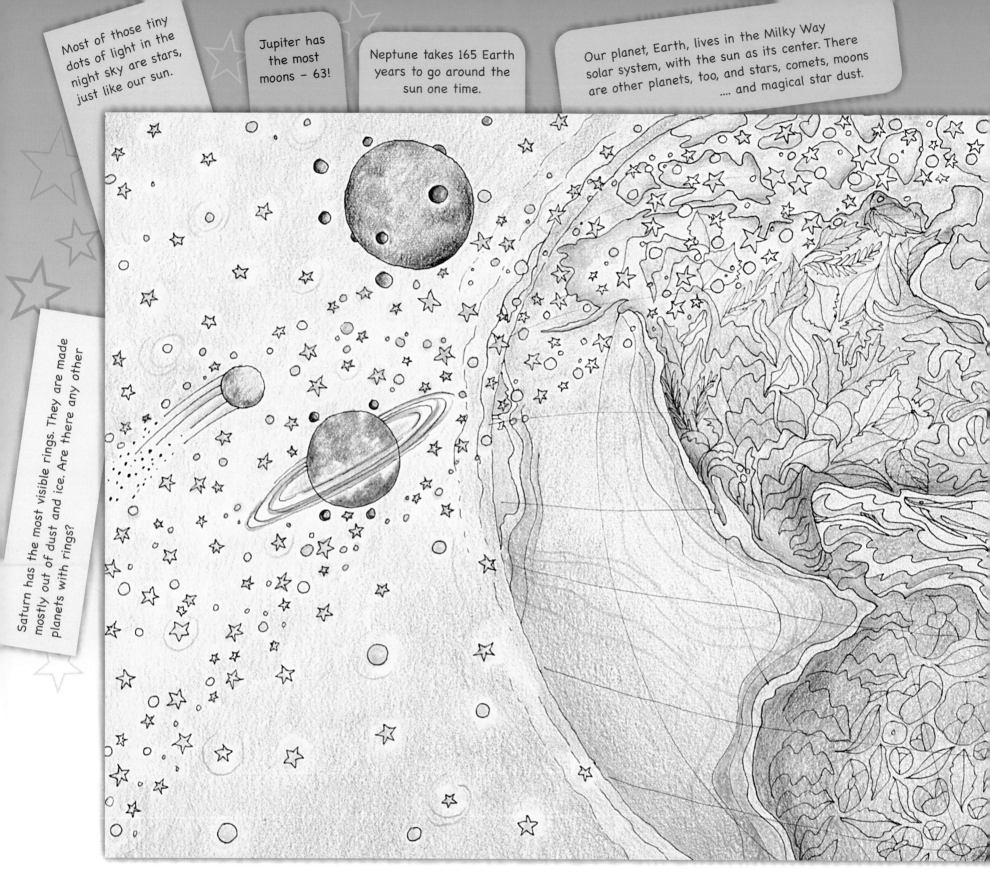

Most of those tiny dots of light in the night sky are stars, just like our sun.

Jupiter has the most moons – 63!

Neptune takes 165 Earth years to go around the sun one time.

Our planet, Earth, lives in the Milky Way solar system, with the sun as its center. There are other planets, too, and stars, comets, moons .... and magical star dust.

Saturn has the most visible rings. They are made mostly out of dust and ice. Are there any other planets with rings?

I began to realize wise Mother Earth was including me

in one of her ancient stories.

All I had to do was listen inside my heart

and I finally heard the words.

We live on a beautiful ball of life – plants and animals and people, tiny microscopic cells, huge mountains covered with trees and snow, oceans full of creatures that swim and breathe in water. We all depend on each other for a healthy place to live.

Earth has only one moon. It shines at night because the light of the sun reflects off its surface.

Sometimes, the moon comes in front of the sun, which then blocks the light of the sun from shining on the earth. That is called an eclipse.

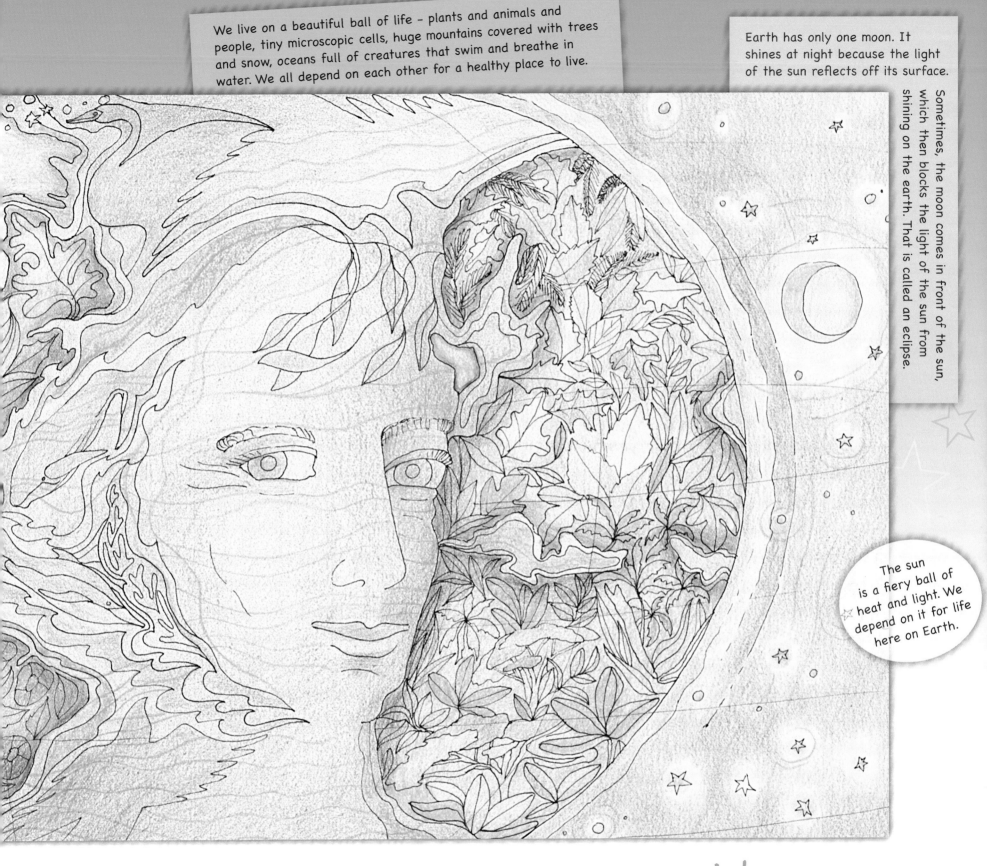

The sun is a fiery ball of heat and light. We depend on it for life here on Earth.

And this is what they said...

Black-Headed Grosbeak has a big, thick beak for crunching seeds. He has one of the most beautiful songs in the woods.

Red-shafted Flicker hunts for insects that burrow into branches and bark. Sometimes, it pecks holes in people houses thinking it is a good place to raise babies!

Great Horned Owl has tufts of feathers that look like horns. Her wings stretch out to six feet!

Robin's nest is made of twigs, grass, and feathers, and lined with mud. She lays as many as 3-5 blue eggs which hatch after 14 days.

Great Crested Flycatcher waits for insects to fly by, then snaps them up for a tasty snack.

Swallows swoop and glide effortlessly.

As in ancient times, the trees grew strong and tall, taller than all the other creatures. And because the Sacred Creator gave all living things gifts, so they were given to the trees.

Great gifts they were, too...

Do you have a favorite bird in your neighborhood? Sometimes they are hard to see, but if you look carefully and stay quiet, you will be able to hear their songs and see their colorful feathers.

Bald Eagle isn't bald. It has pure white feathers on its head.

Canada Geese look for a calm pond to rest and find food. Can you hear them honking?

Squirrels are full of fun and very active. They leap from branch to branch and run up and down the trunk. They can make their homes in holes in the trees, storing nuts and seeds for winter.

Can you count all the birds in this illustration? Don't forget the four hidden ones.

Shelter for busy birds and scampering squirrels...

Fall comes quickly. Maple leaves turn red as the days become shorter, stopping photosynthesis (which uses the energy of light and water to help make leaves green).

Bobcat takes a quick snooze in a space between the roots. It is on the hunt for a rabbit and hoping tonight he will get lucky.

Fox feeds on small animals but often nibbles insects and fruits, too. It needs its fluffy tail to keep warm.

Ants busily work together to gather food and keep a tidy home. Some of the ants are taking care of their queen, who lays eggs that will become ants.

Roots for the homes of burrowing and bunking animals...

singing around the campfire, I glanced over my shoulder across the wildflower
meadow, passed the rock outcropping, and into the smiling trees,
and began to tell the ancient, magical myth about

how the trees got their voices.

We are all connected.

We are all living beings on

an amazing planet. It is up

to us to be guardians of our

beautiful earth and be in awe

of what she provides. Now is

a good time to listen to her

stories in the wind.

More inspiring titles from Satiama, available at Satiama.com!

Children's Spirit Animal Cards by Dr. Steven D. Farmer
Winner of FIVE national awards, these simple yet powerful cards offer children of all ages the opportunity to enjoy beautiful, age-appropriate messages of love and guidance to help them as they develop and grow. Stunningly illustrated, this 24-card deck comes with an enclosed guidebook. Awards include 2012 Sideline Product of the Year and Mom's Choice Gold Medal Award 2011.

Children's Spirit Animal Stories Vol. I, Second Edition by Dr. Steven D. Farmer
A brand new Second Edition of Vol. I stories that now includes original music, sound design and multiple voices! This delightful audio storybook is based on the award-winning Children's Spirit Animal Cards by Dr. Steven D. Farmer, who brings his delightful stories about Arianna and Heather the Hummingbird, Foxy and Secret Favors, Cody the Coyote, and Grandmother Swan.

Children's Spirit Animal Stories, Vol. II by Dr. Steven D. Farmer
Even as our world becomes more complicated, our connection with nature can be restored as we listen to the inner voice that guides us. Like Volume One, this magical audio book, offering stories about Emma the Elephant, Jaden and the Unicorn, Carmella the Caterpillar, and Danny the Dolphin, is a sound and story-telling delight! Music was composed by Grammy award-winning composer Barry Goldstein. Winner of Coalition of Visionary Resources Best Specialty Music/Spoken Word CD, among many others.

Turtle Wisdom Personal Illumination Cards by Donna DeNomme
Awaken the inner child in your adult being! Based on the internationally-acclaimed book, Turtle Wisdom by Donna DeNomme, these cards offer timeless messages of knowing and believing in yourself. The ultimate key is that the wisdom you seek is already within you. A 44-card deck and booklet.

Come Walk With Me: Four Meditation Journeys to Becoming Your Higher Self by Eva Black Tail Swan
Journey is a practice that is becoming more known, understood and used as a mainstream meditation technology for anyone to achieve extraordinary healing – from simple relaxation and relief from stress to relief of pain and more. Cherokee Medicine Elder Eva Black Tail Swan takes her listeners on four guided meditation Journeys – Seeking, Direction, Discovery, and Release and Heal – accompanied by the haunting Native American flute music of Marina Raye.

Safe Passage by Trina Brunk
Throughout Safe Passage, singer-songwriter Trina Brunk offers the gift of music and song to support and ease your journey from the illusion of separation to the reality that Love holds you at the center of your being. The angelic, clear vocals and meditative piano of Safe Passage helps grief and sorrow transmute into courage and hope. For meditation, healing, and ease during major life transitions.

Order any of these products from Satiama.com and use the order code **TREES15**
to receive 15% off these products or any products offered in our online store.
Good for a one-time use only by each customer.

Thank you for sharing our journey!